In her nest there are one . . . two . . .
three baby rabbits!

The baby bunnies hop
around the yard.

Kim hops around the yard, too.
What a funny bunny!

One shy bunny hides as Kim brings water and lettuce.

The sleepy bunnies snuggle close together. Kim snuggles with Carrots, too.

Yvette's Jet

by Sheila Kerwin ❖ Art by Martha Aviles

Little Yvette took off in her jet,
soaring up high in the sky.
She dipped a wing to the crowd below,
and called out, "I love to fly!"

Ladybug, Fly!

by Kelly Bennett
Art by Linda Hill Griffith

Ladybug, ladybug, black and red,
on my hand!

On my head!

Ladybug, ladybug, to and fro,
fly up high,

dip down low.

Ladybug, ladybug—
where did you go?

Grass is green like lettuce.

Rabbits nibble the grass.
Not me!

I run through it.

My toes are ticklish!

Look at Bailey roll!

Merry-Go-Round

by David Rowan ❀ Art by Lynne Avril

Merry-go-round, my favorite ride,
High upon a horse, Daddy by my side.

The music starts. The horses go
Up and down, high and low!

Faster and faster the horses fly.
Wave to Mommy as I gallop by!

The music stops, the ride is done.
Get back in line for more merry-go-fun!

LET'S EXPLORE

Around and Around

Can you make something spin around and around? A pinwheel, a top, or vacuum cleaner wheels?

by Ariel Halback

What makes you spin and twirl?
A merry-go-round, tricycle wheels . . .
. . . or a good friend? *Wheee!*

Clever Crawler
by Sheila Kerwin
Art by Doug Roy
Little caterpillar, in the summer heat–
where do you go with all those feet?